John V.

RAIN PLAYER

To Mum and Dad

PHOTOGRAPHY OF CUT-PAPER ILLUSTRATIONS BY LEE SALSBERY
The preparation of the artwork is described in the Author's Note on the concluding page. The text type is ITC Korinna.

Clarion Books
a Houghton Mifflin Company imprint
215 Park Avenue South, New York, NY 10003
Text and illustrations copyright © 1991 by David Wisniewski

Library of Congress Cataloging-in-Publication Data
Wisniewski, David.   Rain player / by David Wisniewski.   p.   cm.   Summary: To bring rain to his thirsty village, Pik challenges the rain god to a game of pok-a-tok.   ISBN 0-395-55112-9   1. Mayas —Juvenile fiction. [1. Mayas—Fiction. 2. Indians of Central America—Fiction. 3. Games—Fiction.]   I. Title.   PZ7.W78036Rai 1991   [E]—dc20   90-44101   CIP   AC

HOR 10 9 8 7 6 5 4 3 2 1

RAIN PLAYER

STORY AND PICTURES BY DAVID WISNIEWSKI

CLARION BOOKS · NEW YORK

The city lay in darkness, yet the *Ah Kin Mai* had been awake for hours. Trembling, the old priest consulted his charts and calendars once again. "*Kintunyaabil*," they declared. "A year of terrible drought."

The sky reddened and the blazing face of Lord Sun appeared. Without rain, his dreadful heat would soon devour the corn. And without corn, the people would perish.

The *Ah Kin Mai* blew a long clear note on his conch shell. The people had to know their fate. Perhaps Chac, the god of rain, would also hear and have mercy.

On the ball court, Pik played *pok-a-tok* with his friends. Like his father, who competed before the supreme ruler in full costume, Pik had great skill. He blocked a pass with his shoulder and sent the ball flying through the stone ring above his head. "Game!" he cried.

"Hush!" warned the others. "Listen!"

The call of the *Ah Kin Mai* floated in the dusty air. The boys ran to hear what fate the new year would bring.

Pik listened impatiently to the prophecy. "Do the gods have nothing better to do than torment us?" he whispered to his companions. "Things would be different if I were the Ah Kin Mai. I would just tell Chac to get to work!"

The boys' laughter was cut short by a chorus of croaking. The little frogs of the forest, the *uo*, filled the trees about them. Knowing *uo* to be the heralds of Chac, the boys fled. But before Pik could take a step, he was whisked into the swirling clouds above.

The voice of Chac rumbled like thunder. "Is it right for such a small creature to bear such a large tongue?"

Pik bowed before the rain god. "O Mighty Chac, I misspoke," he said politely. "I beg your forgiveness."

"Forgiveness must be earned," Chac replied.

Pik thought quickly. "May I earn it playing *pok-a-tok*? That is what I do best!"

"You wish to challenge *me*?" boomed Chac.

Pik nodded nervously.

"Very well!" Chac agreed. "Two days hence, we shall play. Bring a team, if you can find one. Two games of three shall decide your fate."

"What if I win?" Pik asked.

"You will earn my forgiveness and rain for your people," Chac replied.

"And if I lose?"

Chac laughed and the air smelled like lightning. "You will become a frog and croak my name forever."

"But I don't want to be a frog!" wailed Pik.

"You should have thought of that before insulting Chac," said his father sternly. "Challenging a god to *pok-a-tok*! No wonder your friends refuse to join your team."

"Won't you?" Pik asked hopefully.

"No, I will not," his father replied. "Much more than skill is required." He emptied the contents of a leather pouch onto a table. "At your *hetzmek*, these things were placed in your baby hands: a planting stick, to make the hole for the corn seed, and a ball—"

"To make me a great player!" Pik interrupted. "It has done so!"

"But there is more," his father chided. "Here is a jaguar tooth, that you might share Jaguar's fierce strength. And here is a quetzal feather, that you might receive Quetzal's silent speed. And, most precious of all, the water of the sacred *cenote*, that you might make its deep wisdom your own. Seek their counsel. Perhaps they will know how to help you."

Rising early, Pik came upon Jaguar by first light. "*Otzilen*," he said respectfully. "I have need."

"Indeed," replied Jaguar, inspecting his claws. "All the forest knows of your plight. Fate is against you, but a victory over Chac would give us rain, and that is something we sorely need. I will help you if I can."

"But how?"

"Doesn't your father wear a jaguar cloak when he plays before royalty? Tomorrow, I will be your cloak. More than that, I do not know."

At noon, Pik searched the trees for sign of Quetzal. "*Otzilen!*" he cried. "I have need!"

Quetzal lit upon a branch and regarded him kindly. "I have heard of your challenge to Chac," she said. "Fate is harder than stone, yet it must be broken for the rains to come. I will help you if I can."

"How?" asked Pik.

"Doesn't your father wear a fancy headdress when he plays before royalty? My beautiful feathers will be your crown. More than that, I do not know."

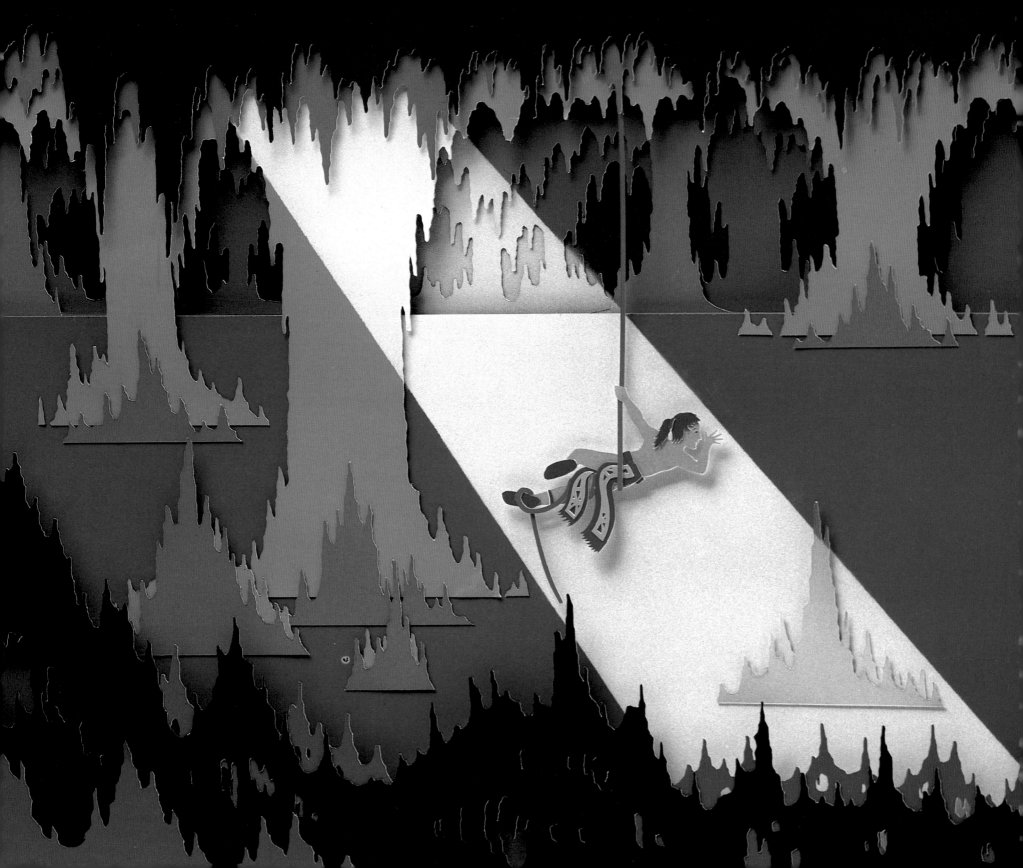

As the sun set, Pik lowered himself into the darkness of the sacred *cenote*. Far below, dark water swirled through the great caves it had carved below the earth. "*Otzilen*," Pik whispered, and his plea echoed in the vastness.

With the faintest breath of air, the words of the *cenote* entered his ear. "I know your step," the *cenote* sighed, "for I flow beneath the ball court. Though fate says otherwise, Chac's rains must continue, for they are my constancy and strength. Go now. Tomorrow, I will be with you."

"But how?" asked Pik.

"Tomorrow," came the echo, and all was still.

The next day, all marveled as Pik strode toward the ball court. A magnificent jaguar cloak hung from his shoulders, and brilliant quetzal feathers streamed from his headdress. Then the people grew silent as the *uo* announced the arrival of Chac in the sky above.

The rain god nodded his readiness to the *Ah Kin Mai*. With shaking hands, the priest held the ball aloft. "Begin!" he cried, and cast it into the court.

A great gust of wind stole the ball from Pik, and a twisting column of cloud blasted it down the court. Chac had sent a whirlwind to play for him!

Instantly, Jaguar leaped from Pik's shoulders. Seizing the ball in his powerful jaws, he sped to the other side and soared through the ring.

"One!" shouted Pik.

Again the old priest tossed the ball into play. At that moment, Chac loosed a score of lightning bolts. They fell with blinding fury, tearing the earth and spinning the ball toward the goal.

Quetzal flew from Pik's head and snatched the ball with her talons. Yet the lightning was stronger than she. Still clutching the ball, Quetzal was driven through the ring.

"One for me!" thundered Chac. He came down from the clouds, and his colossal form dwarfed the tallest temples. "Now I will break this tie!"

The ball fell to the court again. Pik scrambled backward as Chac lifted his huge foot. Then, with a terrific crack, the ground gave way, and Chac plunged into the *cenote* below.

Racing skillfully over the broken ground, Pik sent the final goal flying through the center of the ring. "Mine!" he whooped.

Chac lifted himself out of the hole in silence. Without a word, he took Pik in his great hand and soared into the heavens. "You have won, little man," Chac muttered, "and I cannot say that I am pleased. But we had an agreement."

He placed Pik by the enormous gourd that hung from his belt. "Gently now," Chac warned. "Don't flood the world."

Using both hands, Pik tilted the gourd. A great rain gushed from it and fell to the thirsty earth below.

Chac kept his word to Pik that season and for many seasons thereafter.

In time, the fine young ball player with the strength of a jaguar and the speed of a quetzal gained great renown. He became known as Rain Player, for distant thunder greeted his entrance on the court, and gentle showers followed each victory.

AUTHOR'S NOTE

The realm of the Maya comprised 125 square miles, covering portions of what is now Mexico, Belize, Honduras, Guatemala, and El Salvador. The Maya's time of greatest accomplishment (what archeologists call the Classical Period) lasted about six hundred years, from A.D. 300 to 900. Theirs was a majestic and sophisticated culture. Maya architects carved beautiful cities out of one of the most hostile terrains the earth has to offer. Maya astronomers tracked the movements of the sun, moon, and planets (especially Venus) with astounding accuracy, and Maya mathematicians developed the concept of zero.

Because the Maya regarded time itself as holy, their priests created a wonderfully intricate and accurate calendar. An astonishing array of gods carried the days, weeks, months, and years upon their backs as they trudged through eternity, allotting to each time span its particular good or evil fate. This calendar not only kept track of the present, but also made possible vast projections into the future.

It was the duty of the Ah Kin Mai (ah kin MAH-ee) to make these projections, assisted by prophets called *chilans* (chih-LAHNS). Their job was a difficult one. If predicted good failed to occur, the people would lose faith in the prophet. And if an utter calamity like *kintunyaabil* (pronounced kin-toon-YAH-bil, literally meaning "sun intense all year") was forecast, the people simply waited for it to occur. Any attempt to circumvent it would have been considered useless.

A dramatic example of this tacit acceptance of fate occurred during the long decline of Maya civilization, when the warlike Itza tribe from central Mexico dominated the Maya culture. Tayasal, an Itza chiefdom, was resisting conquest by the Spanish. Tayasal fought ferociously until Andres de Avendano, a Franciscan friar traveling with the Spaniards, mastered the Maya calendar and foretold a time of great political change. When this was communicated to the Itza, they stopped resisting and capitulated to the Spanish invaders, believing that no amount of human effort could prevent a prophecy from coming true.

Certain rare individuals had the courage and force of character to defy the accepted idea of destiny. In the Yucatan city of Chichen Itza, the sacred cenote (say-NO-tay) was used for sacrifices to Chac. Victims were thrown in at dawn; if they survived until noon, they were drawn out of the water and asked what the underwater gods had predicted. On one occasion, there were no survivors, and a nobleman, Hunac Ceel, plunged in. When he surfaced, he shouted that he had indeed spoken with the gods and received a prophecy. For this, he was made ruler of Chichen Itza as well as his hometown of Mayapan.

The favorite game of the Maya was *pok-a-tok* (POCK-uh-tock), a fast-moving combination of present-day soccer and basketball, played with a solid rubber ball on a walled court. Opposing teams tried to send the ball through the stone rings above their heads. Hands and feet were not allowed to touch the ball; it had to bounce off padded hips, shoulders, and forearms. The winning team was allowed to collect the jewelry and clothing of the spectators, who quickly ran away once a match was won. Losers received nothing, and sometimes lost their heads as well as the game.

The *hetzmek* is a ceremony performed to welcome a newborn child into the community. The godparents present the three-month-old girl (or four-month-old boy) with nine items the child will use later in life. These include a loom and grinding stone for the girl, and a planting stick and coin for the boy. The child is then held upon the godmother's hip as she walks about the mat that holds the articles. This ceremony is still performed in the Yucatan.

The Maya have a marked respect for the land and animals that support their life. From this high regard comes the word *otzilen* (aht-ZEE-yehn). It means "I have need," and serves as an apology to an animal that has been killed for food or to the ground that has been disturbed for planting. Though the Maya of today are faced with the technologies and institutions of the modern world, this religious consideration of nature remains with them. Even the corn they raise is addressed as "Your Grace."

Some artistic license has been used in constructing this original story from Maya history and legend. It is highly unlikely that Jaguar and Quetzal (KEHTS-ahl) would be found in the same area as the cenote. While jaguars roamed a good deal of the Maya kingdom, quetzals were found only in the southern highlands. And cenotes occurred only in the Yucatan, where the porous ground absorbs the rainfall into underground rivers that erode the limestone above them, forming a natural well.

The pictures were first drawn on layout paper in pencil, then drawn more tightly with a technical pen on tracing paper. This tracing acted as my guide for constructing the final art. Each portion was transferred to the back of colored papers with carbon paper, then cut out with a #11 X-Acto blade. The pieces were assembled with double-stick photo mountings and foam tape. The finished artwork was then photographed, with each piece lit to provide the most dramatic shadows.